For Raechele, who can never
have too much snow!
— J.C.

tiger tales
5 River Road, Suite 128, Wilton, CT 06897
Published in the United States 2019
Originally published in Great Britain 2019
by Little Tiger Press Ltd.
Text and illustrations copyright © 2019 Jane Chapman
Visit Jane Chapman at www.ChapmanandWarnes.com
ISBN-13: 978-1-68010-157-7
ISBN-10: 1-68010-157-9
Printed in China
LTP/1400/2655/0219
10 9 8 7 6 5 4 3 2 1

For more insight and activities, visit us at www.tigertalesbooks.com

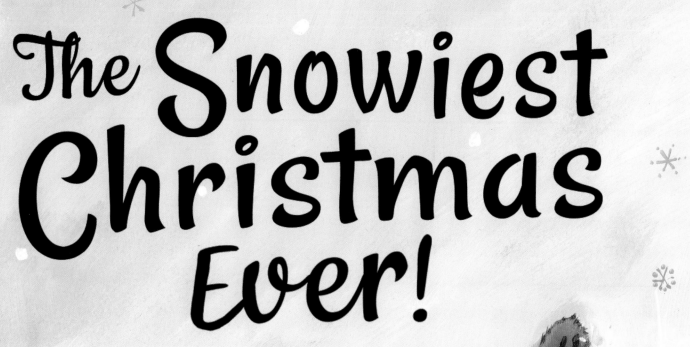

The Snowiest Christmas Ever!

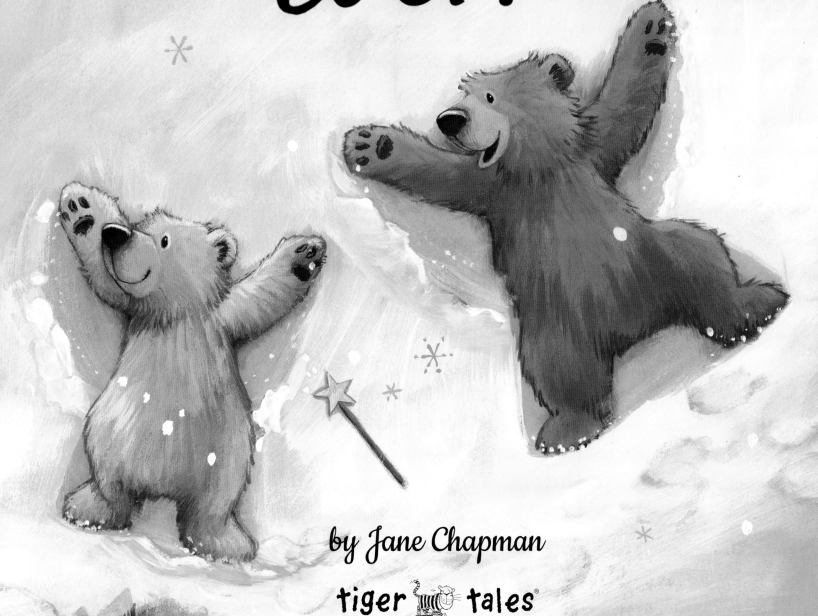

by Jane Chapman

tiger tales

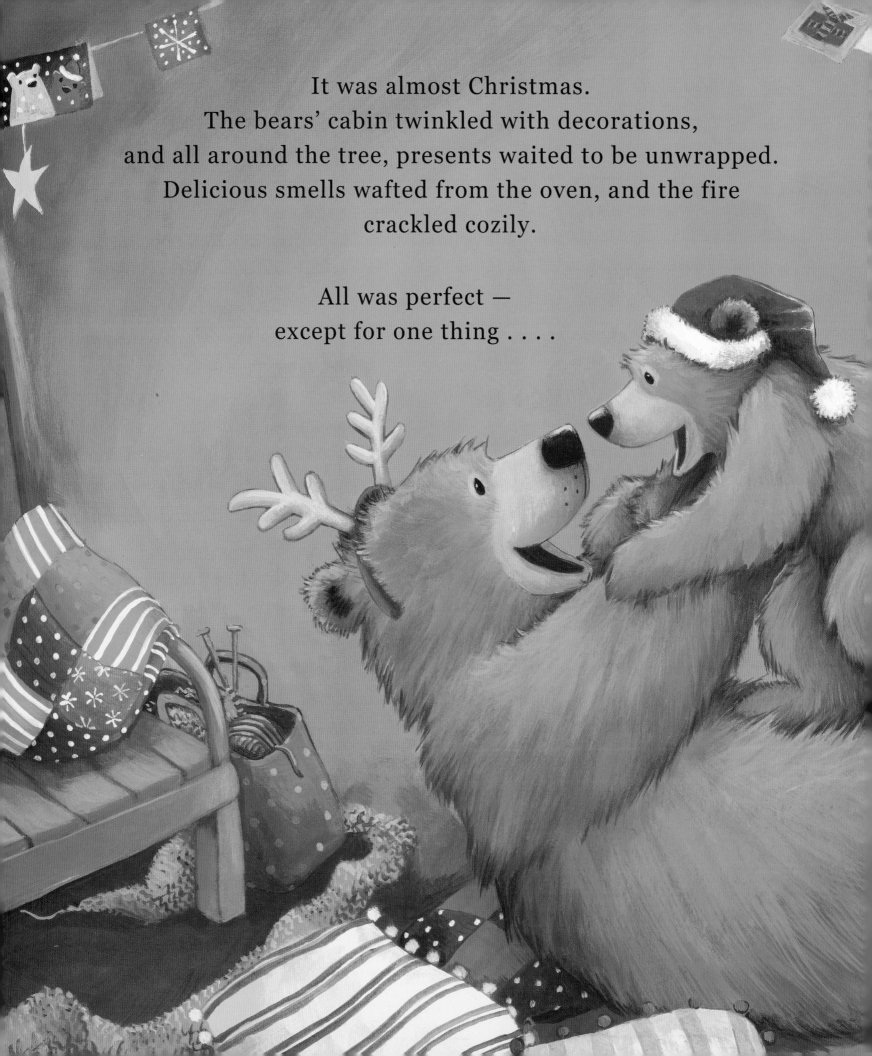

It was almost Christmas.
The bears' cabin twinkled with decorations,
and all around the tree, presents waited to be unwrapped.
Delicious smells wafted from the oven, and the fire
crackled cozily.

All was perfect —
except for one thing . . . .

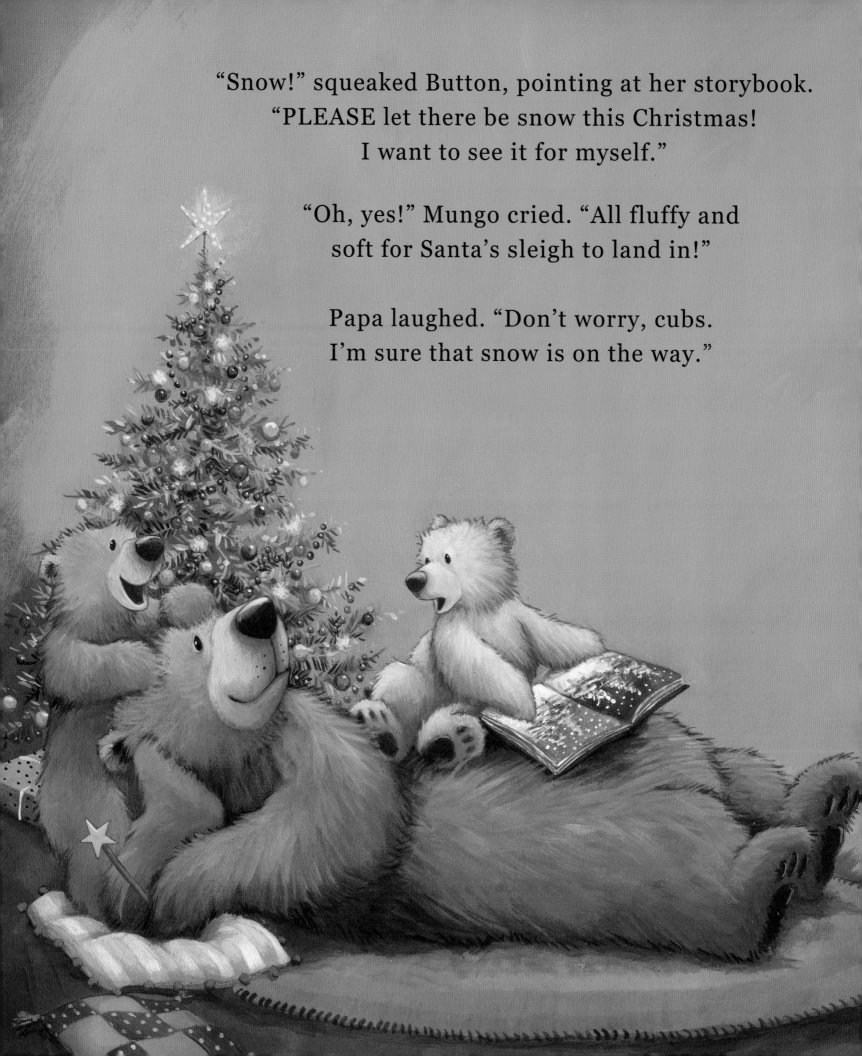

"Snow!" squeaked Button, pointing at her storybook.
"PLEASE let there be snow this Christmas!
I want to see it for myself."

"Oh, yes!" Mungo cried. "All fluffy and
soft for Santa's sleigh to land in!"

Papa laughed. "Don't worry, cubs.
I'm sure that snow is on the way."

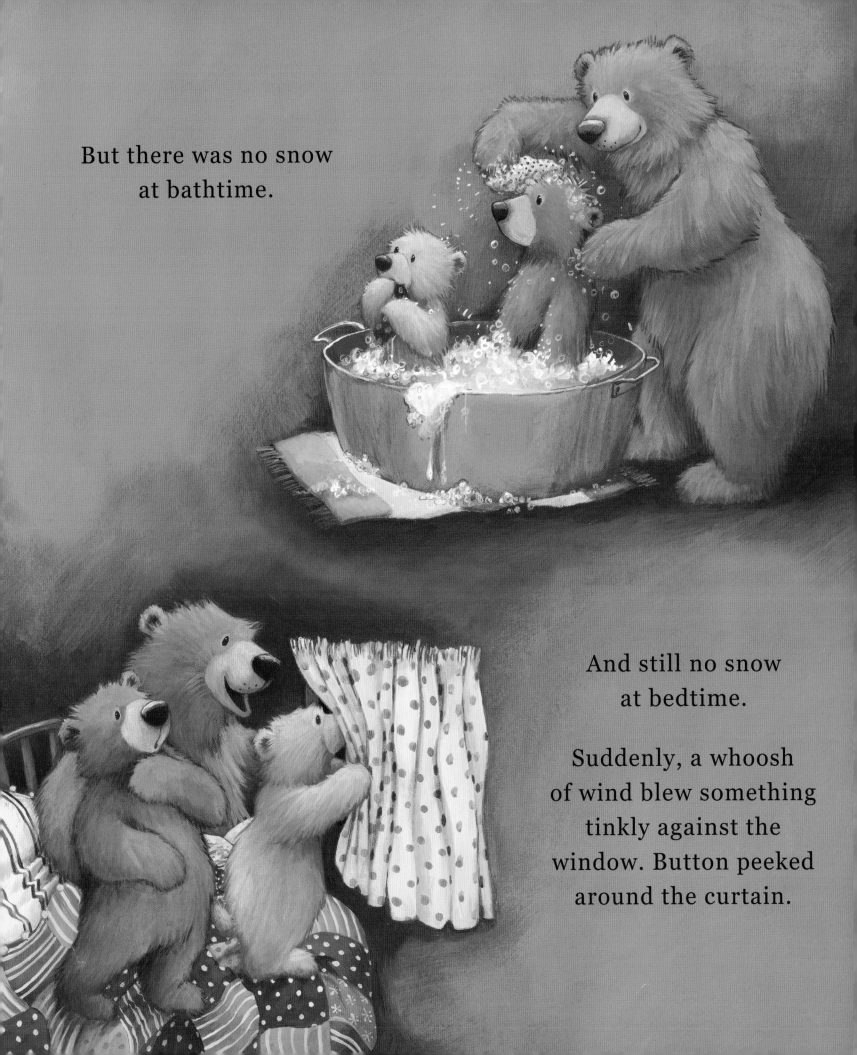

But there was no snow
at bathtime.

And still no snow
at bedtime.

Suddenly, a whoosh
of wind blew something
tinkly against the
window. Button peeked
around the curtain.

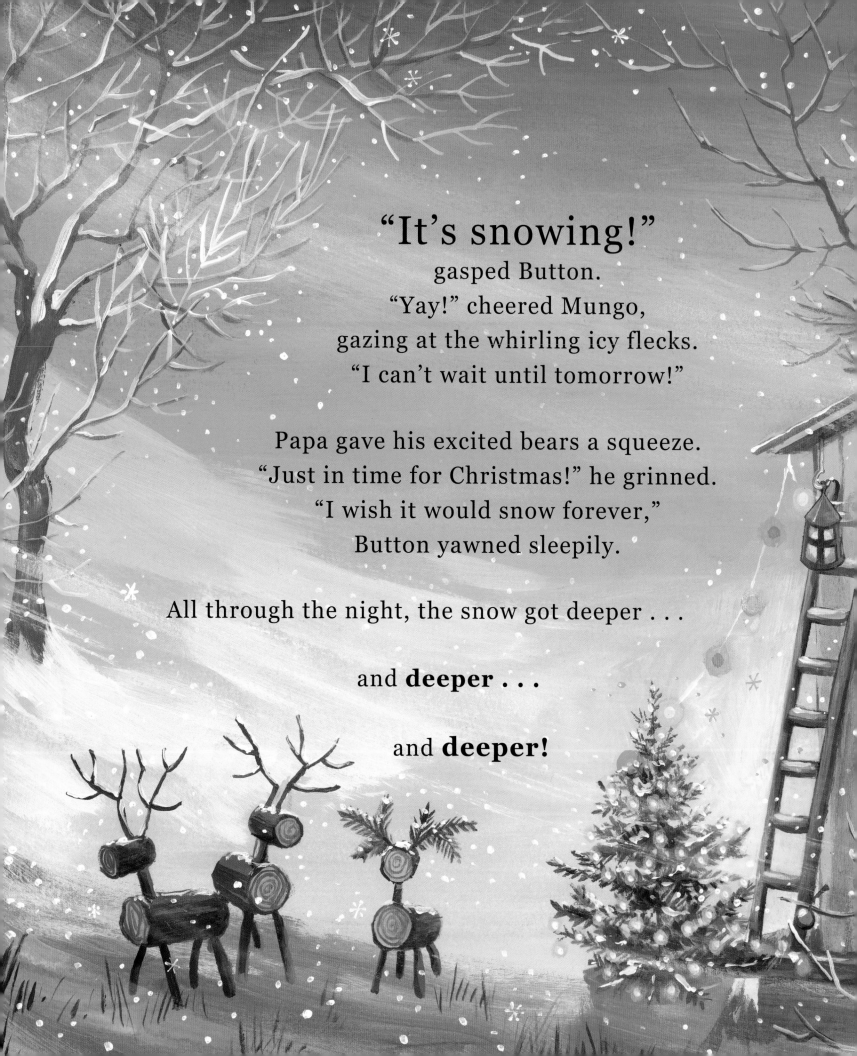

"It's snowing!"
gasped Button.
"Yay!" cheered Mungo,
gazing at the whirling icy flecks.
"I can't wait until tomorrow!"

Papa gave his excited bears a squeeze.
"Just in time for Christmas!" he grinned.
"I wish it would snow forever,"
Button yawned sleepily.

All through the night, the snow got deeper . . .

and **deeper** . . .

and **deeper!**

The next morning, the family heard something
falling onto the rug inside the door.

Plop!

"Christmas cards?" wondered Papa.
"I'll get them!" Mungo shouted,
racing off.

But Mungo was in for a big surprise.
"Whoa! Button, look at this!"

A mound of snow had fallen through the
mail slot. "Ooo!" Button whispered.
"Oh, my!" exclaimed Papa. "I've never
seen snow do THAT before!"

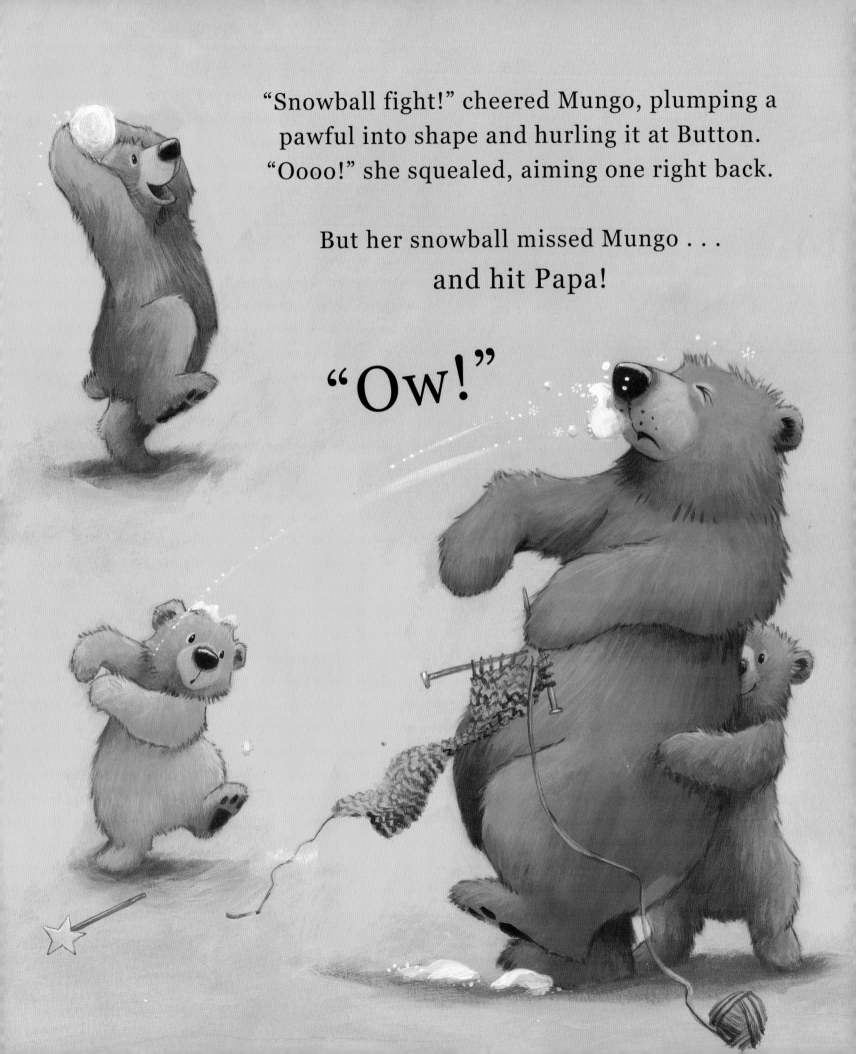

"Snowball fight!" cheered Mungo, plumping a pawful into shape and hurling it at Button. "Oooo!" she squealed, aiming one right back.

But her snowball missed Mungo . . .
and hit Papa!

"Ow!"

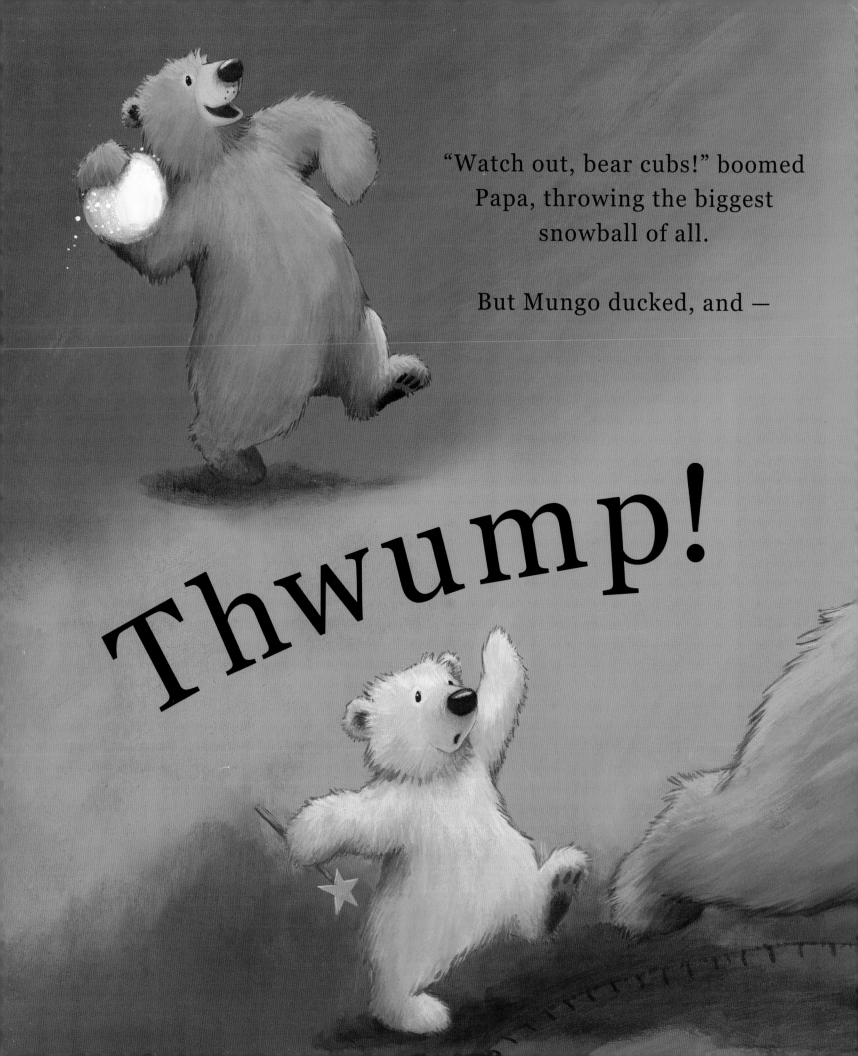

"Watch out, bear cubs!" boomed Papa, throwing the biggest snowball of all.

But Mungo ducked, and —

Thwump!

— Papa's huge snowball hit the Christmas tree!

"Oops!" he chuckled, leaping to grab the tree.
"No more indoor snowballs for us!
Anyone want a snack?"

"This will be the best Christmas ever," mumbled Mungo with his mouth full.

"And the snowiest!" giggled Button, finishing her muffin. "Let's go out and play!"

But Button couldn't open the door.

Neither could Mungo.

"We'll climb out the window,"
decided Mungo. "Come on, Button!"
He jumped up to pull the
handle, and . . .

Flump!

An avalanche of white tumbled in!

"Woohoo! I have a great idea!" grinned Mungo,
and he began to roll a ball of snow around the floor.
Button joined in, paws patting and eyes widening as the
snowball got bigger and bigger.

"We need a carrot, Papa!" called Mungo.
"Still hungry?" replied Papa.

"No, it's for the snowman!" laughed Button.
"Oh, my! An indoor snowman?" exclaimed Papa.
"Quick, cubs, let's clean this up before he melts
into an enormous puddle!"

The snowflakes drifted down all
morning, and long into the afternoon.
"More snow! More snow!"
sang the bear cubs.

Just then, there was a rumble
from the chimney.
"Is that Santa already?" asked Button.
"It's not nighttime yet . . . ."
"Quick! Downstairs!" shouted Mungo.
But when they got there . . .

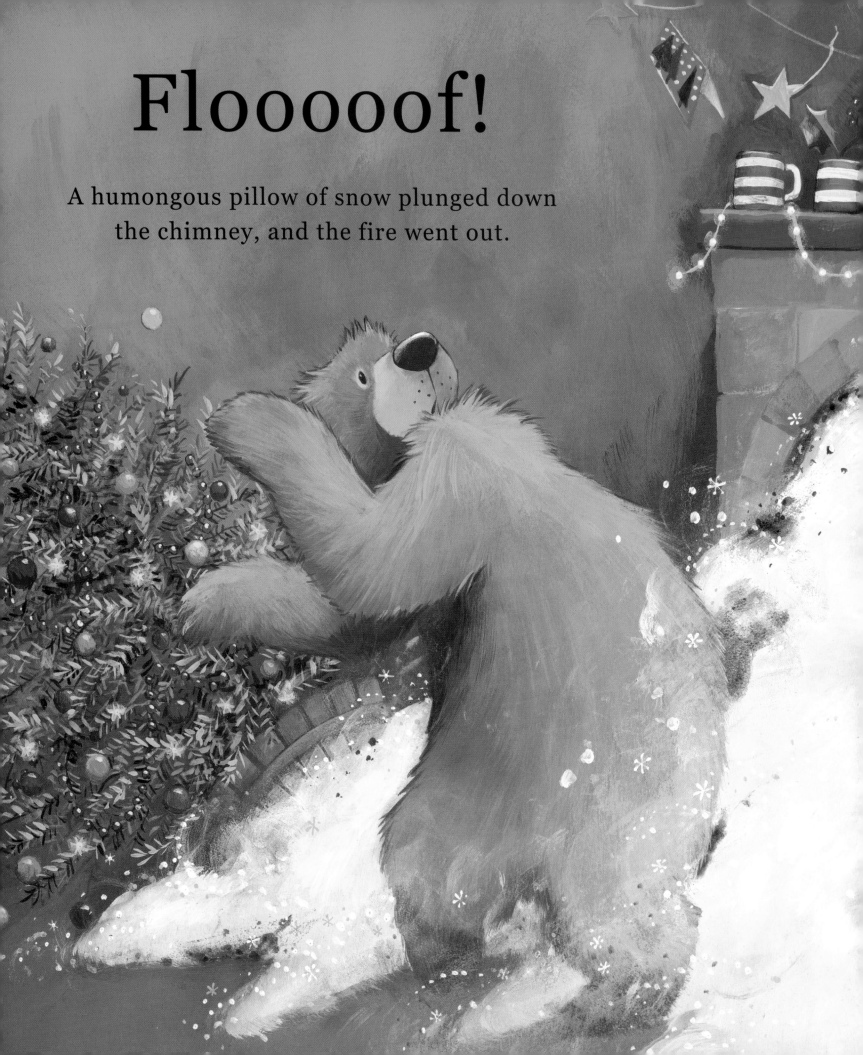

Flooooof!

A humongous pillow of snow plunged down
the chimney, and the fire went out.

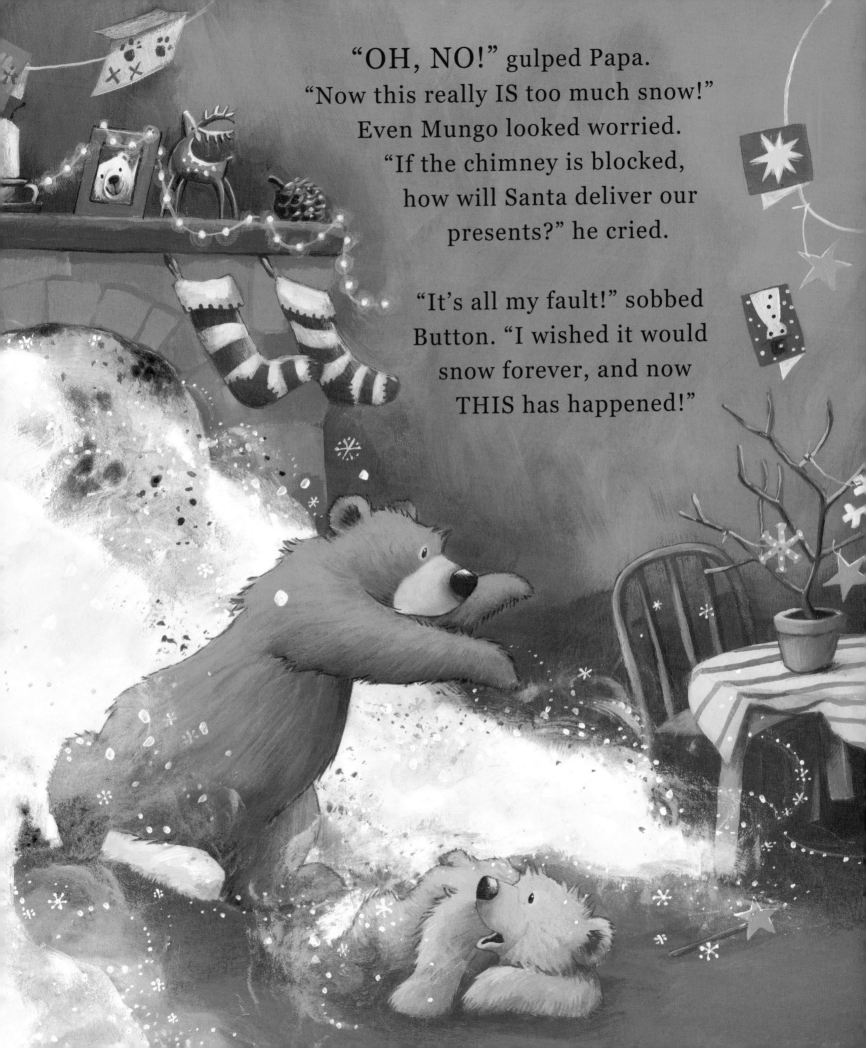

"OH, NO!" gulped Papa.
"Now this really IS too much snow!"
Even Mungo looked worried.
"If the chimney is blocked,
how will Santa deliver our
presents?" he cried.

"It's all my fault!" sobbed
Button. "I wished it would
snow forever, and now
THIS has happened!"

"Don't worry," comforted Papa, gathering up Button in his big bear paws. "We'll help Santa get through!"

"We could use the broom," Mungo suggested.

"Great idea!" agreed Papa.
He squeezed himself into the
sooty chimney and pushed the
broom up as far as he could.

But even on tiptoe,
he couldn't reach the top.

"We'll help, won't we
Button?" announced
Mungo.

So the bear cubs climbed
up onto Papa's shoulders,
and with a wriggle and
a heave . . .

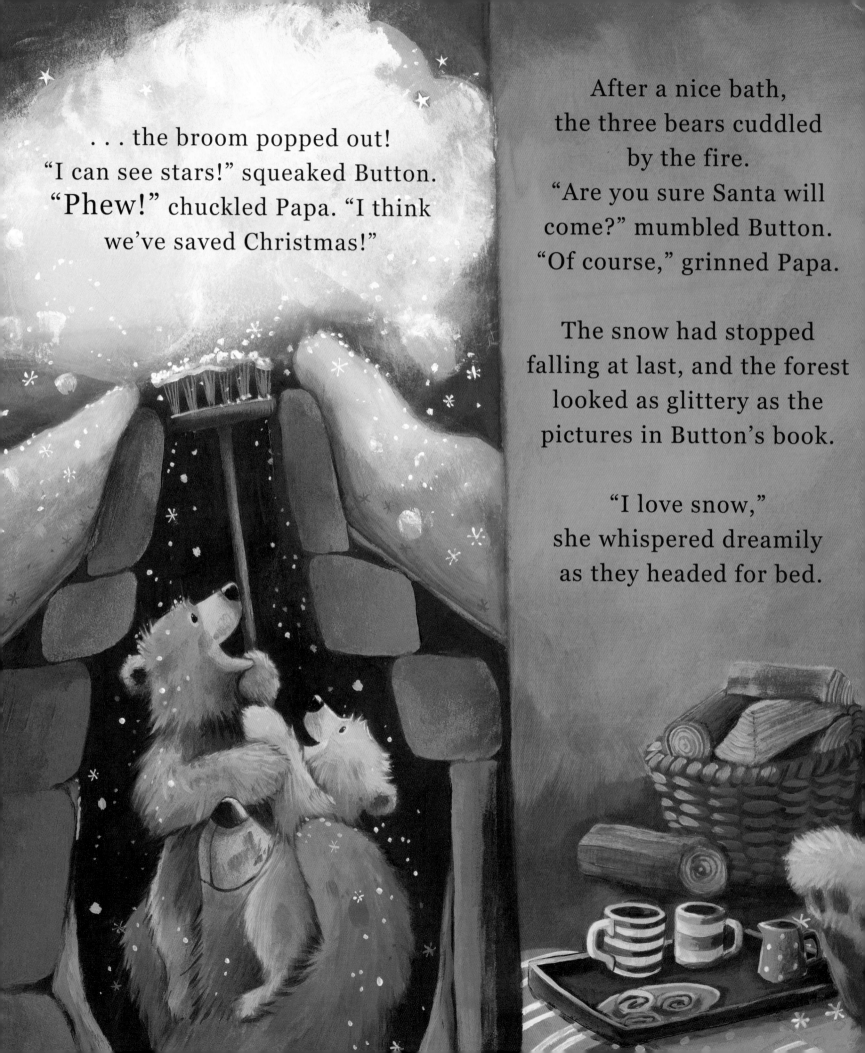

. . . the broom popped out!
"I can see stars!" squeaked Button.
"Phew!" chuckled Papa. "I think
we've saved Christmas!"

After a nice bath,
the three bears cuddled
by the fire.
"Are you sure Santa will
come?" mumbled Button.
"Of course," grinned Papa.

The snow had stopped
falling at last, and the forest
looked as glittery as the
pictures in Button's book.

"I love snow,"
she whispered dreamily
as they headed for bed.

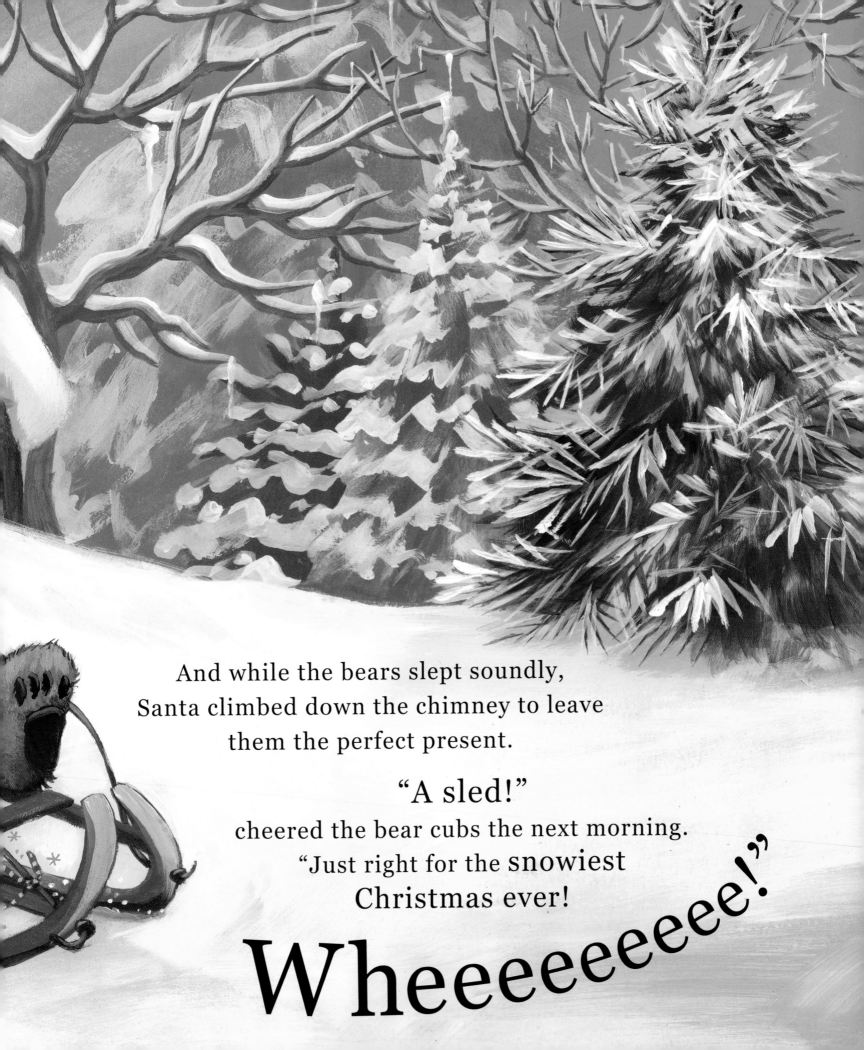

And while the bears slept soundly,
Santa climbed down the chimney to leave
them the perfect present.

"A sled!"
cheered the bear cubs the next morning.
"Just right for the snowiest
Christmas ever!

Wheeeeeeeee!"